# Delilah
### and the
## DishWasher Dogs

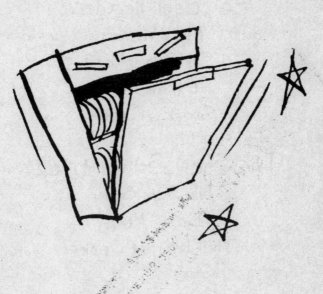

# Also by Jenny Nimmo

Delilah and the Dogspell
Delilah Alone
Hot Dog, Cool Cat
Seth and the Strangers
Ill Will, Well Nell
Tatty Apple

## For older readers
Milo's Wolves
The Rinaldi Ring
Ultramarine
Griffin's Castle

## The Snow Spider trilogy
The Snow Spider
Emlyn's Moon
The Chestnut Soldier

# Jenny Nimmo

# Delilah
and the
# Dishwasher Dogs

Illustrated by
Ben Cort

Mammoth

For my son Ianto,
who gave me the idea,
with love

First published in Great Britain 1993
by Methuen Children's Books Ltd
Reissued 2001 by Mammoth
an imprint of Egmont Children's Books Limited
a division of Egmont Holding Limited
239 Kensington High Street, London, W8 6SA

Text copyright © 1993 Jenny Nimmo
Illustrations copyright © 1993 Ben Cort
Cover illustration copyright © 2001 Chris Priestley

The moral rights of the author, illustrator and cover illustrator have been asserted

ISBN 0 7497 4559 2

10 9 8 7 6 5 4 3 2

A CIP catalogue record for this title is available from the British Library

Printed and bound in Great Britain
by Cox & Wyman Ltd, Reading, Berkshire

# Contents

# 1

# A Broken Heart and a Tiger's Skin

It is just after midnight on a moonless Monday. A cat leaps on to the Watkins' wall. It is Delilah, queen of the night-garden. She is huge with wild smoky grey fur and whiskers like long needles of silver. Her flame-gold eyes beam into the dark, searching for the movements of mice. 'Misty,' she murmurs in disgust. 'I can't stand bad weather.'

This is answered by a tiny sound that seems to come from her feet and something moves in her great shadow. A small black kitten has scrambled up beside her.

'Tudor, I want you to find me a rat,' says Delilah. 'You don't have to kill it. Just find one and I'll do the rest. There's a whole family in the orchard at the bottom of my Edward's garden.'

Tudor regards the dark, endless spaces of the night and gives a regretful mew. 'I can't,' he says. 'There are THINGS out there.'

'Nonsense,' says Delilah. 'Nothing you can't handle. It's time you grew up. I can't do your hunting for ever.' Secretly, she is worried about Tudor and wonders if she has brought him up properly. He is her foster-kitten but she feels responsible. He is too timid, easily frightened and far too slow. Other kittens snigger behind his back and call him names. Delilah feels ashamed for him.

'Go on,' she says. 'Now!'

Tudor looks up at his foster mother: wise and beautiful, she is truly a queen. He would do anything for her, but not this. Not a pounce into nowhere, into places where monsters lurk. 'I can't,' he says.

Delilah glares at him furiously, but a distant sound distracts her. She runs to the end of the wall and sits on a pillar overlooking the street. Tudor follows and peeps over her tail.

A strange vehicle comes rolling towards them. It looks like an ice cream van, but it is not. It comes to a halt, right in front of the cats, almost as though it has been drawn to them and cannot break away. Its engine throbs ominously and a bitter-smelling cloud drifts from the exhaust. There are no pictures of tasty pink and yellow ices on the side, no rose and lime-green lollies, not even the hint

8

of a chocolate and nut cornet. Instead there are silver moons, golden stars and a broken heart pierced with an arrow. There is a man in a pale hat like an upturned pudding-bowl; he is supporting a gun almost as tall as himself and, half-hidden in the long grass behind him are two yellow eyes and a set of sharp white teeth.

Everything about this van is threatening. Tudor is rigid with fright. His eyes fix themselves on the broken heart and the words above it that he cannot read.

# BIANCA LOVES BERTRAM FOR EVER!

If the cats could see or understand the words on the other side of the van they would learn that the driver is a fortune-teller and that her name is Bianca Bono.

But Delilah doesn't need words to tell her what she wants to know. She can read the message in the pictures perfectly.

From the window of the driver's seat, Bianca Bono glares at Delilah. She has tiny black eyes and a swirl of white hair. Bianca hates all cats. Her husband, Bertram Bono, was eaten by a tiger and she has sworn to take her revenge on every cat in the world. But first she must capture Delilah. Delilah, queen of the night-garden. For Delilah can shrink dogs, and a dog is Bianca's secret weapon.

'So you're the one,' mutters the fortune-teller. 'The one they call queen of cats. Witch! Dog-shrinker! I'll get you!' And as she drives away she sobs, 'Bertram, my darling, you'll be avenged, I promise you!'

Delilah growls after the van and then both cats see something that is far more frightening and terrible than the strange pictures and the white-haired woman. Stretched across the back of the van is the skin of a huge striped animal. This awful sight reminds Tudor of the creatures he sometimes sees in his dreams of another life. Creatures he might have known and even loved.

'What does it all mean, Mama?' he asks.

'It means,' she says, 'that someone has killed a tiger, that someone has been eaten by a tiger and that someone else has a broken heart. It also means that cats had better watch out!'

'Why, Mama? Cats are not tigers.'

'True!' Delilah gives the kitten a lick of approval. 'Cats are not tigers. Not quite. Nevertheless they had better watch out. We'll give hunting a miss tonight. Go home now, and stay there!'

# 2

# Tabby-Jack

On that same dark night, Bianca Bono came creeping down Pandy High Street. She wore a hooded cloak made of very dark purple stuff, and floaty black trousers that could have been pyjamas, but were not. She also wore gold sandals over black socks.

She swooped towards shop windows, peering in, and then winged off again. When she reached Dex-Electrics, however, she stopped and gazed upon the vast array of shining white machines with an air of triumph. Looking furtively over her right and then her left shoulder, she sidled towards the door. This was made of thick glass, threaded with a criss-cross pattern of tiny wires. Bianca took a small gold card from the pocket of her diaphanous trousers and, turning her back on the glass door, she quickly scanned the upper

windows of the houses opposite. Not a light anywhere. Not a soul stirring. Everyone was asleep. Everyone but Tabby-Jack, across the street, lying on a sofa in the window of Daybreak Fabrics and looking like a stuffed toy cat.

Tabby-Jack watched the door of Dex-Electrics swing open. He didn't move but his grey-green eyes grew round and his shoulders stiffened. The tall woman made a flourish with fingers that resembled candles dipped in gold.

The alarm bell was silent and the door

closed behind the swift, floating figure.

Tabby-Jack leapt from the daisy-covered sofa and ran through the dark shop. A velvet curtain hung behind the counter, concealing the storeroom. Tabby-Jack crept beneath the curtain and glided past rolls of fabric and tall pillars of wallpaper until he reached the back door. At the bottom of the door his owner, Dilys Daybreak, had thoughtfully inserted a cat-flap. Tap-tap! The cat-flap rattled through the silence as Tabby-Jack jumped into the back yard. He rocketed down an alley, and straight across the High Street, casting caution and kerb drill to the wind. Down the path beside Dex-Electrics he sped, ignoring the mice poised upon mountains of cardboard, waiting to die. For Tabby-Jack was a notorious hunter.

But the big tom cat was thinking only of Rose, Rose of the fine white fur and melting fern-green eyes, Rose who lived above Dex-Electrics with old Mr Dexter. Tabby-Jack knew the woman with gold-tipped fingers was up to no good. Her furtive floatiness was wicked, her long fingers were sinister and her spicy, dangerous scent made Tabby-Jack feel dizzy. When he reached the yard behind the shop, he had to negotiate a forest of boxes, tins, tubes and polythene before he could get to the window, and then he found that it was too high for him. He jumped on to the dustbin and poked his head, very cautiously, forward until he could see into the back room.

There she was! The stranger had thrown back her hood and a thin light from something she held, illumined a pale face and hair as white as Rose's fine cat fur, but not as shiny. The stranger's hair was dead-white cloudy stuff without any life at all. Tabby-Jack's spine tingled as though someone had run an ice cube down his back. He withdrew his head to get his thoughts in shape, then leant forward with a little more daring.

White-hair was peering at the labels on the dishwashers. She beamed a small torch across the lines of writing, scrutinising every letter. She was searching for something in the way that Tabby-Jack inspected the grass for the flutter of a mouse. At last she seemed to have found what she wanted. A gleeful expression passed over her face and her lips rolled back revealing a row of rock-like teeth, long and yellow like a dog's.

Tabby-Jack held in the growl that bubbled at the back of his throat. Could this be a human being? He craned his body perilously further over the edge of the dustbin; he had to see what the stranger would do next, Rose's life might be at stake.

The white-haired woman knelt beside one of the dishwashers. She couldn't restrain a soft giggle as the machine swung open. From the folds of her dark cloak she drew out a handful of something. One hand beamed the torch on to the bony, upturned fist of the other, almost as though she were going to do a magic trick and throw a bunch of flowers in the air. She looked very pleased with herself. Slowly she uncurled her fingers and there, on her crinkly, pale palm, were two tiny creatures. They were as small as grasshoppers but they were dogs. Tabby-Jack was sure of it. He would have known a dog anywhere, even if it was an inch high. But these dogs could not be real. Their faces showed nothing. Their eyes were fixed and glazed and their hair was flat and shiny. They must be magic.

Holding the dogs as though a shiver might break them, White-hair carefully placed them inside the dishwasher. Then she did something with her dangerous fingers; she twisted and fiddled with the door of the

machine before she closed it. The door snapped shut and the woman threw back her head. Such a malicious sound came cackling through her long dog's teeth, Tabby-Jack began to lose his balance. As his claws scrabbled desperately on the dustbin lid he found himself looking into the pinprick black eyes of the stranger. She had seen him!

With a squeal of fright Tabby-Jack slid off the dustbin and the heavy lid clanged in an endless roll as he tore into the dark. He could hear the swift padding of footsteps behind him, he could feel the whirl of a cloak stirring the night air and he could smell the spicy scent pursuing him. Tabby-Jack had seen something he should not have seen, and he wished he had not. Now his own skin was dearer to him than Rose's snowy fur. He ran faster than he ever dreamt he could. Terror of the whirling white-haired creature made his paws leap and bound as though the ground were burning him. But he couldn't escape her. He raced down secret alleys, under fences, over railings; he flew across empty streets and silent gardens, but she was always there, just behind him.

He found himself in a district he knew well. His friend, Tudor the kitten, lived here, in a warm house with a cat-flap always open. But the gate was shut and Tabby-Jack's strength was failing. He leapt and leapt again. He mewed, 'Tudor! Help me! Quickly!' He called for as long as he dared before a figure came billowing round the corner towards him.

A window opened and Annie Watkin looked out. 'Is that you, Tabby-Jack?' she called. 'You woke me up. What is it?'

But Tabby-Jack had gone and Annie only saw something dark, wrapped in a gust of wind, sweep down the street and disappear.

# 3

# The Dishwasher Arrives

Tudor heard Tabby-Jack's cry for help. But Delilah had told him to stay at home. He heard Annie call out to Tabby-Jack and wondered if he should disobey Delilah and go out into the night; if it were only to prove to himself that he was not afraid.

Annie looked cross when she came down to the kitchen next morning. She dropped the milk and forgot to give Tudor his breakfast. 'I hate being woken up in the middle of the night,' she said.

Tudor tried to tell her about the missed breakfast, but Edward Pugh from next door came in and said, 'Hurray for half term. Come on, Annie, let's go for a ride.'

Annie brightened up. 'OK,' she said.

Tudor hoped he might get a meal from Mrs Watkin when she came in, but no such luck. Annie carried him outside and plonked him in her bicycle basket. 'I'm going to give Tudor an experience,' she told Edward, 'to make him brave.'

Tudor cowered in the basket while Annie and Edward wheeled their bicycles down to the field behind the houses. It began to rain.

Things could hardly get worse for Tudor, but they did.

Rain didn't worry Edward. He was trying out his new mountain bike; twenty-one speed, cantilever brakes, padded saddle and down tube bottle and cage. 'King Edward of the road,' he cried as he bounced over a dead branch.

Annie tried to overtake but her front wheel smashed into the branch and Annie toppled into a nasty mixture of cowpat and mud.

Tudor flew out of the basket and raced for the trees.

Edward heard the accident and looked back. He tried not to laugh but the effort was too great; he shook so much he fell off his own bike and he couldn't tell Annie that Tudor was making for the trees.

'Shut up!' yelled Annie. She felt awful. The bike had bruised her leg and horrible browny-green slime had oozed down her neck and into her wellingtons. Worst of all, she smelled disgusting.

'Tudor!' Edward managed at last. 'He's running away.'

'Oh, no!' wailed Annie, pulling herself out of the mud.

'I'll find him,' Edward said kindly. 'You'd better go home and get cleaned up.'

Annie turned away without saying thank you. She blamed Edward for the mess she was in. He had asked her to come out just so that he could show off his new bike.

She tramped back along the track, extremely sorry for herself, and by the time she reached home she had worked herself into such an indignant and vengeful state she had quite forgotten to cry.

'Annie, whatever . . .' exclaimed her mother.

'It was Edward's fault,' said Annie, her lower lip beginning to tremble.

'How?' Mrs Watkin didn't look as troubled as she should have been.

'He was doing silly things,' Annie grumbled, wondering why her mother looked so cheerful. 'I need a bath.'

'I should think you do. Drop your clothes right there. Wait, I'll get some newspaper.' Mrs Watkin went to a cupboard while Annie began to pull off her wellingtons. It was only when she stood, sadly contemplating her filthy white socks, that she noticed something had happened in the kitchen.

A brand-new dishwasher had been installed. It was slotted neatly between the oven and the sink. So that's why Annie's muddiness hadn't bothered her mother.

'It came then,' said Annie, eyeing the dishwasher as Mrs Watkin cast newspaper round her feet.

'Isn't it beautiful?' said Mrs Watkin happily.

'I wouldn't call it beautiful,' commented Annie. 'Useful, I suppose.' She dropped soggy garments on to the paper. 'Can I load it sometimes?'

Mrs Watkin mumbled, 'Mmm,' rather reluctantly. It was a new toy, Annie concluded, so she had better not play with it until her mother had got used to it. She tiptoed over the kitchen floor in her vest and pants and ran upstairs for a set of clean clothes. When she came down again her mother was busily scrubbing the jeans in the sink and Edward was sitting at the table, eating a bun. Tudor was curled up in his lap.

'I found him,' Edward told Annie in what she considered an unnecessarily boastful tone.

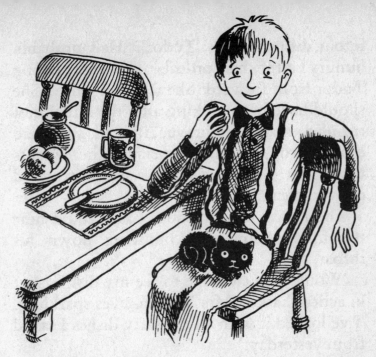

'Thanks,' Annie managed somewhat grudgingly.

'We're having a new dishwasher, too,' said Edward.

'I know.' Mrs Watkin scrubbed contentedly. 'We chose them together, your mum and I. They delivered yours right after ours, while you and Annie were having fun in the field.'

'Annie wasn't having fun,' Edward tittered.

Annie glowered. She took a tin of Smashcat from a shelf, opened it and spooned the meat into a dish marked, 'Tudor'. 'He's probably hungry after his ordeal,' she said taking Tudor from Edward. She felt a bit guilty. She should have been looking after the kitten, not trying to make him brave. After all, she'd had quite a struggle trying to persuade her parents to get him. But he was still so small, so scared of everything.

The kitten was ravenous. You could hear the food sliding and bumping down his throat.

'Would you two like to see my dishwasher in action?' asked Mrs Watkin, eyes sparkling. 'I've loaded it with all the dirty dishes I saved from yesterday.'

'Yes, please,' Edward said politely. He knew how pleasant it was to show off new things.

'Here goes! First time ever!' Mrs Watkin selected a programme, turned a switch and pressed a button. 'Bingo!'

Nothing happened for a second and then there was a trickling sound. Tudor stopped eating and looked at the dishwasher. The trickling sound became a buzz and then a rumble.

'There!' Mrs Watkin was ecstatic.

Not so Tudor. His ears flat against his

head, he tore under the table, then round the kitchen, flinging himself at places that might have provided cover if only he was clever enough to open them. In the end, he found a shopping bag on the floor and crawled into it.

'What's he frightened of?' asked Edward.

'The dishwasher,' cried Annie. 'Stop it, Mum!'

'I couldn't possibly,' said Mrs Watkin. 'It's in the middle of its programme. That kitten will just have to get used to it.'

Mr Watkin walked in, wearing his trainers, personal stereo and headphones.

27

'The dishwasher's working, Harry,' Mrs Watkin shouted.

'Ah,' murmured Mr Watkin without enthusiasm. 'I'm off for a run.'

At that moment Tudor shot out of the bag and clung to Mr Watkin's leg. His claws were small but as sharp as thorns.

'Ahhhhh!' screamed Mr Watkin, trying to see what had burned him. He was so tall he had great trouble in seeing things near the floor, especially if they were small. He ran and opened the back door to cool off his leg and Tudor leapt away into the garden.

'Phew!' said Mr Watkin. 'What was that?'

'Tudor,' said Annie, peering out. 'He's terrified. There's something funny about the dishwasher.'

'That kitten's afraid of his own shadow,' Edward remarked. 'Machines have never bothered Delilah.'

'Tudor's different,' cried Annie. 'He's got a sixth sense. He *knows* something, that we don't.'

# 4

## Delilah's Visitors

Hidden between a clump of daisies and the Watkins' wall, Tudor was trembling like a leaf. He had just heard dogs growling in Mrs Watkin's new dishwasher.

Why hadn't Mrs Watkin heard them? Why hadn't Annie? Or didn't they mind having animals in their machine?

Tudor was frightened of dogs, even pass-you-in-the-street, bark-worse-than-bite type of dogs. But the animals hiding in Mrs Watkin's grim white machine were hell-bent kitten-crunchers, raging famished cat-munchers. He was sure of this. They were the monsters who lurked in the dark spaces of the night, waiting to catch him.

Tudor let out a tiny mew of distress and it was this sound that led Tabby-Jack to his hiding place.

'What's up?' Tabby-Jack called through the daisies.

'Catastrophe!' mewed Tudor. 'Dire, awesome, calamity!' He had learned these words from Delilah. Her vocabulary was prodigious.

'What has happened?' demanded Tabby-Jack.

'There are dogs in Mrs Watkin's new machine,' Tudor whispered.

'You don't say.' Tabby-Jack pushed his way through the plants and squeezed into a space beside Tudor.

'The Watkins can't hear them,' said Tudor. 'I don't understand.'

'Humans are practically deaf,' said Tabby-Jack. 'They can't even hear a sparrow these days.'

The little kitten began to mumble incoherently. Sounds like 'cruncher, muncher, bone and masher,' slipped between his small first teeth.

'Calm down,' said Tabby-Jack. 'This is all very interesting. I think we have stumbled on a mystery.' And he told Tudor about the extraordinary events of the previous evening. 'I managed to escape the dreadful creature after a while,' went on Tabby-Jack. 'But it was touch and go. I was too exhausted even to climb over your gate. I thought you might get Annie to rescue me. Didn't you hear me calling?'

'Er – no.' Tudor looked away and then asked quickly, 'Did you say the woman put *tiny* dogs in the dishwasher? The voices I heard were enormous.'

'Strange. Let's tell Delilah,' Tabby-Jack suggested. 'She'll know what to do.'

'Of course!' Tudor had been so frightened he hadn't even thought of Delilah. He had wanted only to hide.

They crept through the secret hole that Annie and Edward had made in the wall dividing their gardens, and walked round to the Pughs' back door. 'Dee-li-laah!' they called through the cat-flap.

'Buzz off!' said Mrs Pugh from inside.

Undeterred, the cats persisted. 'Deee-li-laah!'

The back door opened and a wicked-looking shoe appeared.

'Did you hear me?' said Mrs Pugh. 'Stop that caterwauling.'

Tails down, cat and kitten walked out into the garden and looked up at Delilah's special window. There she was, a mound of smoky-grey, glaring at the rain with angry golden eyes.

Tabby-Jack and Tudor raised their heads and stretched their necks. 'Deeee–li–laaaah!' they called again. Tabby-Jack pitched his voice so high Tudor had to lean away from it and he wasn't surprised when a rotten apple came flying through the kitchen window. It just missed Tabby-Jack's left ear. 'That woman is definitely not cat-friendly,' complained the tabby cat.

They ran for Mrs Pugh's front porch and sat on the mat, hoping she wouldn't guess where they were. They had just scratched the mat about a bit to make it comfortable when a ginger paw appeared at the top of the gate. There was a 'click' as the gate came unlatched and opened.

'Jerome,' sighed Tabby-Jack. 'What does he want?'

Jerome was Tabby-Jack's brother but they were not alike. To tell the truth Tabby-Jack was jealous of Jerome, for he was larger, stronger and definitely more spectacular. He lived with Mrs Daybreak's brother Harold who ran the Sauce-boat café. Harold was not fond of cats and had only taken Jerome to please his sister. Jerome lived off scraps and rats and slept in a cold box in Harold's back yard. To make up for his unhappy home life he was rather bossy and boastful. Worst of all, he was trying to win the heart of Rose Dex-Electrics. If he succeeded Tabby-Jack would have to leave the district. He loved Rose so much he would not be able to endure the sight of her and Jerome together.

'Hi!' said Jerome, swaggering up the path.

'What are *you* doing here?' asked Tabby-Jack.

'I might ask *you* the same question,' said Jerome. He had no intention of telling his brother the reason for his visit. Rose had not answered his calls that morning and he

34

wanted to ask Delilah's advice about it. He came and made a place for himself on the mat. Tudor, squashed between the two big toms, began to feel breathless.

'We've come to see Delilah,' Tudor panted. 'On a very urgent matter. There are dogs in Mrs Watkin's dishwasher.'

'Tell all!' Jerome gave a purr of interest.

Tudor looked at Tabby-Jack. 'Most of it happened to him,' he said.

After a moment's hesitation Tabby-Jack launched himself into his story, emphasising his own bravery and the frightening aspect of the white-haired woman.

'A woman with dog's teeth,' Jerome exclaimed. 'Magical dogs. In Dex-Electrics. Why didn't you call me? Two cats are better than one and we've got Rose to think of.'

'I managed very well on my own,' snorted Tabby-Jack.

'But Rose . . .'

Tudor felt Tabby-Jack's muscles tighten.

'She admires me, you know,' Jerome continued. 'I wouldn't like anything to happen to her.'

A low hiss escaped Tabby-Jack.

They sat in silence, watching clouds of rain drift across the Pughs' immaculate lawn.

Tudor felt even more uncomfortable between the two hostile brothers. He was trying to think of something soothing to say to them when he heard the soft patter of paws on the path beside the house. A huge grey head appeared and two golden eyes stared into the porch.

'Mama!' cried Tudor, bounding up to his foster-mother.

Delilah endured his grapple for a moment before scrambling under cover and shaking out her long wet fur. The others retreated without complaint. Delilah was queen of the district, a most remarkable cat whom even humans respected. It was rumoured that she was a witch. She could certainly shrink dogs. Jerome had seen her do it.

'This looks like a committee meeting,' observed Delilah. They could not tell if she disapproved, she had such a very regal way of talking.

'More of a delegation,' said Jerome. 'Tudor, tell Delilah!'

Tudor could see that Tabby-Jack was still in a bit of a huff so he told his story for him. 'The white-haired woman must have put the tiny dogs in the dishwasher delivered to Mrs Watkin,' Tudor said. 'But the dogs have

36

grown inside the machine, Mama. Their growls are terrible.'

Delilah sat back, spread her foot like a star and cleaned between her toes. Tudor knew that this did not indicate a lack of interest on Delilah's part. On the contrary her mind was working furiously. At length she said, 'There's a connection. I have no doubt whatever that these dog noises have something to do with a tiger and a broken heart. But what?'

The two toms looked bewildered.

'Show me the dishwasher,' Delilah said,

without giving away her thoughts.

'Yes, Mama. Thank you!' Tudor said.

The front door opened and Mrs Pugh looked down on the four cats. 'You again!' she said. 'Delilah, if you must invite half the neighbourhood round, will you kindly take them into someone else's garden. Preferably his!' She pointed an accusing finger at Tudor.

Delilah swore so softly only Tudor heard it. Then she lifted her nose and marched away. The other cats followed rapidly.

'That Delilah,' muttered Mrs Pugh. 'Who does she think she is?' She was tempted to slam the door but was worried about the stained glass panel and had to content herself with a firm but gentle 'clunk'.

As the cats approached the Watkins' house, Jerome coughed nervously and asked, 'Delilah, could you tell us what all this has got to do with tigers?'

'I don't know yet, do I?' snapped the majestic cat. 'But we shall soon see, shall we not?'

And Jerome, who had a reputation to consider, fluffed up his tail and tried to look fierce.

# 5

# Trapped!

Edward had made himself comfortable in the Watkins' kitchen. He liked it better than his own because it was more homely. Annie's mother enjoyed company when she was cooking, while his own mother was always shooing him out.

Mrs Watkin had just made some cinnamon cookies. They smelled delicious and Edward was hoping that he would be invited to try one.

'Do you like cinnamon cookies?' asked Annie, reading his mind.

Edward was about to answer when Delilah jumped through the cat-flap, closely followed by Tudor and a neat tabby; last of all came a huge ginger tom. They walked over to the dishwasher and sat in a row in front of it.

'Well!' said Mrs Watkin, at a loss.

'That's Tabby-Jack,' said Annie. 'Dilys Daybreak's cat. He was howling outside last night. I'm sure it was him. But when I called him he vanished.'

Mr Watkin came in, singing. He peered at the cats and said, 'They look as though they're in the front stalls, waiting for an opera to begin. What *do* they want?'

Annie said, 'Something in the dishwasher, I think.'

'Look at Delilah!' Edward exclaimed. 'Her ears are all poked forward as if she is listening to something.'

Everyone was quiet, trying to hear what Delilah was listening to. But all they heard was Mrs Pugh calling, 'Yoo-hoo!'

'Come in, Grizelda,' shouted Mrs Watkin. 'We're in the kitchen.'

The first thing Mrs Pugh saw, on opening the back door, was a row of cats. 'Good Lord, Pam,' she said. 'How can you stand it? Those toms look really vicious.'

'Try a cinnamon cookie, Grizelda,' Mrs Watkin said quickly. 'Can I help you?'

'Oh.' Mrs Pugh was confused. 'I've got your dishwasher, Pam. The label with your name and address is still on it.'

'It doesn't matter, Grizelda. We chose the same models at the same time, didn't we? In fact we've got the same machines. So we

don't need to exchange them, do we?'

Mrs Pugh blushed. 'How silly of me.'

'Let's go and have a quiet coffee in the sitting-room,' suggested Mrs Watkin.

Edward wondered if quiet coffees were different from other coffees. He noticed that Annie had one of her investigating moods coming on. Her forehead had screwed itself into deep furrows of concentration.

When the children were alone, Edward said, 'What's up?'

'The dishwasher,' said Annie in a hushed voice. 'Delilah knows that this one was meant for her.'

'But they're both exactly the same,' Edward argued.

'No, there's something different about this one. Tudor was afraid of it just now. I think he's brought the others in to inspect it. And Tabby-Jack knows something. He was calling out last night in a very frightened way. He's Tudor's best friend, you know.'

'Let's go out and think,' Edward suggested. 'It's stopped raining.'

'I'll tell Mum we're getting her a paper. You never know, there might be a clue in it.'

Before they left, Edward looked back at Delilah. For some reason he was very

reluctant to leave her. He couldn't explain this feeling even to himself, let alone Annie. He hesitated. No, he was being silly. Of course Delilah would be all right. She was a sensible and clever cat.

When the cats were alone they moved closer to the dishwasher. Jerome inserted a paw and pulled the door down.

Now they could see the gleaming interior. Mrs Watkin had emptied the machine and the cats gazed at their reflections in the shiny walls. There was not a sign of dogs.

'They were *very small*,' said Tabby-Jack,

trying to explain their absence.

'Invisible?' asked Jerome.

'No. They sort of shone.'

'A trick,' stated Delilah. 'I'm going in to investigate.'

'But, Mama . . .' cried Tudor.

Delilah fixed him with a cool golden stare. 'You want me to get to the bottom of this, don't you? You want me to find out about the growls, don't you?'

'Yes, but . . .'

'You'll never be able to eat your breakfast in peace if this goes on, and it follows that I shan't be able to eat mine in peace either.'

Tudor looked down at his paws. Delilah was quite right, of course, but he hated it when she drew attention to his weakness. He knew she was trying to make him grow up, but it made him feel ashamed.

'Listen,' said Delilah. 'I'm going in and when I'm in I want you to close the dishwasher tight. Got it?'

'Suppose we can't open it again,' Tabby-Jack asked sensibly.

'Fetch Annie!'

'She's out.' Tudor began to panic.

'Mrs Watkin, then,' Delilah said impatiently. She jumped on to the door of the dishwasher and crept neatly between the vertical plate supports. 'Now!' she commanded. 'Close the door.'

Jerome and Tabby-Jack looked at each other and then at Tudor.

'Now,' hissed Delilah, 'before anyone comes back.'

The three cats outside the dishwasher closed their eyes, put one paw each on the door and pushed. There was a loud smacking sound and Delilah was locked in.

'I take my hat off to Delilah,' said Tabby-Jack, 'I've never met such bravery.'

'I was trapped in a washing-machine,' sniffed Jerome. 'When I was a kitten,' he added.

'That was stupidity, not bravery,' said Tabby-Jack with a scornful look at his brother.

Tudor's legs began to shake so violently they nearly gave way. 'Mama!' he squeaked.

'Pull yourself together,' said Jerome. 'She's not your mama, for one thing, and it's time you grew up, for another. Be a tom!'

'He's not ready for that,' Tabby-Jack defended Tudor. 'Now I suggest we're all very quiet. Something might be happening in there.'

If something was happening in the dishwasher, they couldn't hear it. They waited for what seemed an eternity until Tabby-Jack remarked that Delilah hadn't told them how long to wait before they opened the door.

'Oh, let's try now,' cried Tudor.

The brothers stood on their hind legs and pressed the handle. Nothing happened.

'Meeeeeooooow!' wailed Tudor.

Mrs Watkin looked in. 'Whatever is it?' she said.

'I'll shoo them out,' said Mrs Pugh, following her into the kitchen. She kicked out with her pointed shoe. Jerome and Tabby-Jack backed towards the door. Jerome growled and spat at her.

'You nasty, vicious thing. Get out!' shouted Mrs Pugh.

Jerome and Tabby-Jack leapt through the cat-flap.

'Really, Pam. I don't know how you can stand it. I couldn't abide strays in my house.'

'I don't think they're strays, Grizelda,' Mrs Watkin protested mildly. 'Their coats look very nice.'

'All the same I'd have one of those special magnetic cat-flaps fitted, like we have for

Delilah. They only let your own cat through.'

Tudor could not contain himself. He mewed round Mrs Watkin's legs, begging her to open the dishwasher.

'I'll just pop the cups in the dishwasher,' said Mrs Watkin, as if she had understood the kitten. She tugged. She turned a knob and pulled. 'Grizelda,' she wailed. 'It won't open.'

Mrs Pugh had a go. Without success.

Mrs Watkin ran to get her husband. Mr Watkin had a go. He couldn't open the machine either. 'I'm not mechanical,' he explained.

Tudor flung himself at the dishwasher with

an ear-splitting shriek.

Mrs Pugh glanced at the kitten with distaste. 'I suggest you ring Dex-Electrics,' she said. 'Their machines are guaranteed. They'll have to come and open it. I expect they've got special tools.'

'Oh, dear, my lovely, brand-new dishwasher.' Mrs Watkin was almost in tears when she ran to the telephone.

The cats looked at each other, aghast. Then Tudor wailed, 'It's the tiger skin woman. Her magic dogs have eaten my mama!'

'No,' said Tabby-Jack, trying to keep calm. 'The dogs were much too small to eat a cat. But Delilah's trapped, that's for sure!'

# 6

# Bianca in Disguise

Edward and Annie were just returning from the newsagent's when a white van drew up outside Annie's house and a very peculiar person got out of it. They could not tell if it was a man or a woman because, although it wore a check cap, its white hair was rather long, and beneath its brown overall, gold sandals and floaty black trousers could be glimpsed. The person gave the children a nasty sneer as it sneaked past them, and ran up the path to Annie's door where it put a bony finger on the door bell.

'Are you expecting visitors?' asked Edward.

'I don't think so,' Annie said.

'Who is that, then, a long-lost uncle?'

'Hardly,' Annie said indignantly.

Mrs Watkin opened the door and Bianca Bono said, 'Having trouble with your dishwasher, dear?' Her voice could not be

identified as either male or female. She had disguised her voice and she sounded as though she were chewing iron bars.

'How quick!' exclaimed the delighted Mrs Watkin. 'I've hardly put the phone down.'

'I was conveniently just round the corner,' said Bianca. 'Mr Dexter linked me up on the car-phone.'

'Wonderful.' Mrs Watkin stood aside to let Bianca in. Annie and Edward followed, fascinated.

Tudor was now quite beside himself. He

was howling round the kitchen like a cat in a nightmare. Mrs Pugh was trying to drive him out by clapping her hands and stamping her feet. Mr and Mrs Watkin were too concerned about their dishwasher to pay much attention to the kitten.

'Ah, yes.' Bianca cracked her knuckles and prodded various buttons on the machine. Then she bent down and listened. An expression of something like joy passed over her horrible face and she said, 'We'll have to take it away, dear.'

'But . . .' said Mrs Watkin.

At that moment Tabby-Jack leapt through the cat-flap, snarling; Jerome followed, spitting like a fire-cracker.

Bianca turned on them with a screech. 'Back!' she yelled. 'You beastly brutes. You horrible, verminous animals.' This was said with such malicious savagery the others could only stare at her in stunned amazement.

'That's a mean . . .' Edward began.

'Shut up!' shrieked Bianca, grabbing a broom. 'Here!' Sensing an ally she handed the broom to Mrs Pugh. 'Keep them back while I get this thing out.'

Mrs Pugh was only too delighted. The spitting cats were driven into a corner while

Bianca tugged the dishwasher into the middle of the kitchen.

'Can I help?' asked Mr Watkin, none too eagerly.

'No!' snapped Bianca. 'I've got my trolley.' And she ran out, presumably to fetch her trolley.

'Doesn't seem very official,' observed Mr Watkin.

'Oh, they send all sorts these days,' Mrs Pugh assured him. 'Those brutes seemed to have calmed down at last,' she added, giving the cats a prod for good measure. She spoke too soon, however, for all at once the two toms made a break for it and began to circle the dishwasher. Tudor joined in and all three ran faster and faster, crying and mewing in despair.

'What's the matter with them?' cried Annie.

'They don't want the dishwasher to leave,' Edward shouted above the racket.

'Don't be silly, Edward,' said his mother, attacking the cats with her broom again. 'Out! Out! Out!' she shrilled.

Mr and Mrs Watkin joined in half-heartedly and the cats were finally driven into the garden.

'I've never known anything like it,' said Mrs Watkin, locking the cat-flap. 'D'you think it's something in the water?'

'Everything has changed,' sighed Mrs Pugh. 'Cats weren't like that when I was a child. They were disciplined.'

Bianca Bono came back with her trolley and began to heave the dishwasher on to it. Mr Watkin helped with ineffective little prods and shoves.

Edward suddenly began to feel sick. 'Where's Delilah, Mum?' he asked. 'She was here when we went out.'

'Goodness knows,' said Mrs Pugh.

'You don't think . . .' He pointed at the dishwasher.

Bianca darted him such a furious look, it took his breath away.

'Delilah's not the sort of cat to go jumping into dishwashers,' said Mrs Pugh.

But when the dishwasher was wheeled away Edward felt compelled to follow and as he walked out of the front door, Tudor and the two toms flew out from nowhere and began to run round Bianca and the dishwasher, hissing, spitting and howling like creatures from a horror story.

Bianca set down her trolley, reached into

her overall pocket and brought out something small which she threw at Tabby-Jack. It landed at his paws with a bang. Tabby-Jack gave a cry of pain and leapt into the air. The other cats had slowed down now and Bianca suddenly attacked them with tiny white pellets, which fizzed, banged and sparkled all around them.

Normal people don't do that, Edward thought, but he was too dumbstruck to move.

It had quite a different effect on Annie. She ran into the shower of explosions, crying, 'You horrible person! Stop it. That's my kitten,' as she gathered Tudor into her arms.

The two toms jumped over the wall and vanished.

'Ha! Ha!' Bianca laughed joyfully, revealing huge yellow teeth. She wiped her hands with satisfaction. 'Dirty beggers,' she said. 'Brutes. They ought to be put down, every last one of them.' And she wheeled her trolley on to the pavement.

'That's not very fair,' murmured Mr Watkin, who had come out just in time to see the last few explosions.

But Bianca just wheeled trolley and dishwasher up a ramp at the back of the van

and slammed the doors. Then she leapt into the driving seat and drove away.

Five minutes later Mr Dexter arrived and asked to see Mrs Watkin's dishwasher.

'It's gone,' said Mrs Watkin. 'Your – er – man came to take it away.'

'Man?' Mr Dexter clamped a hand to his forehead. 'My man's off sick. Someone's stolen your dishwasher, Mrs Watkin. Call the police.'

It was then that Mrs Pugh remembered something rather important. 'You know, the last day or so,' she said, 'I've been followed by someone with gold sandals, just like the ones that thief was wearing. I remember thinking how peculiar it was to wear them on a wet day. It was when we were choosing the dishwashers, Pam.'

Down in the Pughs' orchard, Jerome and Tabby-Jack called to Tudor. But he never came.

'How can humans be so stupid?' moaned Tabby-Jack. 'Don't they know a dangerous woman when they see one? We've got to rescue Delilah before it's too late.'

'She's a match for anyone,' said Jerome. 'Don't forget her dogspells. I saw her working on a Rottweiler last year. What a scene! Sparks everywhere. He ended up looking like a scorched gerbil.'

'But Delilah is powerless against humans,' Tabby-Jack reminded his brother. 'She can only work on dogs.'

'I'd forgotten,' Jerome admitted gloomily. 'In that case we'll have to rescue her. We'll need Tudor; he knows Delilah's scent. I'll get Rose to persuade him. She's wonderful with kittens.'

Tabby-Jack chose to ignore the last remark. He didn't like thinking about Jerome's friendship with Rose. But he agreed to meet his brother in the orchard after dark.

# 7

# Into the Mountains

Tudor couldn't sleep. He sat on the kitchen windowsill and gazed at the vast night sky. He had never imagined what it would be like to miss someone. Something heavy and dark lay inside him and he wondered if it could be the emptiness that Delilah had left behind her. Had she gone for ever, or was there just a chance? Was there something he could do to save her?

He could hear her soft voice in his head. 'Moon-times are good, kitten. Come out into the night. I'll show you how to hunt. How to find things.'

But Tudor was afraid. He was afraid of the hugeness of the night, the wide, dreadful muddle of the world outside his garden, and the terrible creature who had thrown exploding stars at him. Staring miserably at the beckoning glitter in the sky he said, at last, the word that Delilah had cried out when he had run from his first mouse. 'Coward!' she had hissed, and Tudor had known that it was the most despised thing in the world.

'That's what I am,' he mewed, 'a coward.' Unable to restrain himself he cried bitterly, 'Mama! Mama! Mama, why did you go into the machine?'

There was a soft tapping on the cat-flap and when Tudor looked round, fearfully, to see what had entered, there, in a patch of moonlight sat the most beautiful creature he had ever seen. Her fur was whiter than the moon, her eyes like brilliant rain-washed leaves.

Tudor edged along the windowsill, jumped on to a chair and watched the white cat for a moment, then he leapt to the floor. Cautiously he approached the moon-coloured creature; now he could hear her soft purr. He lifted a paw but dared not touch.

'Don't be afraid.' Her voice was like music.

Tudor slipped his head under her chin and purred at the cool silkiness of her fur.

'They told me you'd be frightened,' she said, licking his head. 'So they sent me to fetch you.' She licked his cheeks, his eyelids and his neck. And Tudor felt courage seeping into him. 'They're waiting for you next

door,' the white cat continued. 'We're going to find Delilah.'

'How?' asked Tudor.

'With noses, paws and dream-pictures.'

'Dream-pictures?' Tudor murmured.

'The pictures that tell us where things are, what the weather says and who to be afraid of.'

'Oh, those.' To tell the truth Tudor had not fully developed his dream-pictures. He still got lost and mistook the postman (bad) for the milkman (good).

The white cat stopped licking and looked at

Tudor. 'You are not a tom yet. I know that the world confuses you. But I won't let you get lost. I've had kittens, you see.'

'I think I've heard of you,' said Tudor. 'Are you Rose?'

'I am.' The white cat padded over to the cat-flap and looked back at Tudor. 'Come!' she trilled and stepped neatly into the dark.

For a moment the warm, safe kitchen tugged at the kitten. He looked at his basket with the soft rug Annie had knitted for him. He thought of Delilah, locked away in a cold white machine, starving, perhaps, dying. He had to help. He leapt after Rose with a cry he'd never used before. It sounded bold and eager and made him feel much older.

At the bottom of the Pughs' garden Jerome and Tabby-Jack were waiting under the low branch of an apple tree.

'We're going to find Delilah,' Jerome told the kitten, 'or die in the attempt. We cannot allow a mere human to steal the wisest, most venerable cat in the district. You must come because she is your foster-mother.'

'I understand,' Tudor said nervously. 'But I'm not very big yet and . . .'

'You're afraid, aren't you?' Jerome accused the kitten.

'No,' Tudor protested, 'but will we have to go far?'

'We don't know yet, do we,' Jerome answered impatiently. The responsibility of the operation weighed heavily on him. 'We'll find the white van first. I'll lead the way. I'm used to being out all night.' He glanced at Tabby-Jack. 'Want to walk along with me, Rose?' He gave the white cat a winning look.

A warning grumble came from Tabby-Jack.

But Rose hung back. 'I'll stay with the kitten,' she said.

Tabby-Jack relaxed. Jerome strode out into the fierce moonlight; the others followed, but a soft light high in the Pughs' house caught their attention. Edward was sitting in Delilah's window. He seemed to be staring into the garden but he might have been asleep.

'He's been there all night,' said Tabby-Jack. 'Poor boy, he doesn't know what's become of Delilah. He's very fond of her, you know. I think he's been crying.'

'I wish we could tell him about the dishwasher,' said Tudor.

'He'll find out if he cares enough,' Jerome said with a hint of bitterness, for no one cared for him, not even his owner, and now Rose had declined to walk with him. The big tom marched resolutely across the Pughs' lawn, walked round the house, up the front path and unlatched the gate with his paw. Tabby-Jack followed, Rose and Tudor came last, walking side by side. They passed through the open gate and out on to the pavement. Here, orange-coloured lights hung over them, turning everything to shades of grey. Even the trees looked dead.

As the four cats walked up the mysteriously silent street, Tudor whispered to Rose, 'Do you know Delilah, then?'

'Of course,' said Rose. 'All cats know Delilah. She advises, teaches and defends us.'

'I didn't realise,' said Tudor, wonderingly. 'I thought it was only me.'

They continued in silence until they reached the outskirts of the town. Jerome seemed to know exactly where to go. He turned on to a rough side-road. Here trees grew thickly, right down to the tarmac and there was no smooth pavement to walk on. The road narrowed and rose sharply. A fresh wind raced over the tree-tops, making them moan and rustle.

'We're going into the mountains,' Rose

told Tudor, and there was a tremor of excitement in her voice.

Tudor's legs felt wobbly, his pads were sore and the sharp mountain wind made his eyes water. He had never known pain like this and wondered if it could get worse. He was about to beg for a rest when they turned a bend and found the white van. It was parked in a clearing where the trees receded several feet from the road.

'Interesting,' said Jerome. 'There was an ice cream van here yesterday.'

'How do you know it was an ice cream van?' asked Tabby-Jack.

'It was pink,' snapped Jerome, 'and anyway, I know. Someone always gives me a lick if I hang around those things long enough. Let's have a look.' He jumped on to the bonnet and peered bravely through the windscreen. 'Empty!' he pronounced.

'Are you sure?' The others all spoke together.

'Take a look!'

Rose and Tabby-Jack leapt on the bonnet. 'Gone!' they agreed. Tudor, too small for such a leap, took their word for it. 'This pink van,' he asked tremulously, 'did it have pictures on it?'

'As a matter of fact it did,' Jerome
confessed; 'moons, stars, a tall man and a
broken heart.'

'What was on the back?' Tudor whispered.

'Didn't go round the back,' said Jerome.
'What's up, kitten? You look washed out.'

'It's hers!' Tudor's voice rose. 'The tiger
skin woman. She came down our road last
night and she stopped and looked at Delilah
all sort of . . .' he couldn't describe Bianca's
dreadful expression. 'On the back of the van
there was a . . .' he took a breath, 'a skin of a
dead animal. A beautiful striped animal. And

Delilah told me that someone had killed a tiger and been eaten by a tiger and someone else had a broken heart, so cats had better watch out.'

An appalled silence greeted the kitten's speech. And then Tabby-Jack declared, 'This is even more serious than we imagined. We must hurry.'

'But where to?' asked Rose. 'An ice cream van is hardly likely to go into the mountains.'

'It's not in town, I'd have noticed,' said Jerome. 'So it must be on the motorway.'

'Motorway?' Rose and Tabby-Jack exclaimed in horror.

Tudor had not heard of motorway. It was obviously to be avoided at all costs.

'We won't have to go on the motorway,' Jerome said in a patronising tone. 'We'll walk cross-country. We'll see the pink van easily from above. At least I will. And there's another thing. The white van is still warm from travelling, so perhaps the creature has only just left.'

Tudor wondered if his legs would last. He longed to be picked up by the neck and carried in a gentle mouth. Growing up was proving to be quite exhausting.

Rose knew how he felt. She gave him a few

licks of encouragement and Tudor set off, feeling almost a new kitten.

Travelling over the soft sheep-grazed mountain was easier on the paws. Now the cats ran low and fast, hunting-fashion, and very soon they found themselves on a narrow track that overlooked the motorway.

Tudor gazed on the wide road snaking away as far as he could see, a blur of light and sound. Even now, when the town was fast asleep, this monster was still wide awake. They waited and watched until they noticed an oddly-shaped vehicle trundling below them in the outside lane. It had a row of coloured lights on the roof and it was moving much slower than anything else on the motorway.

'That's it,' cried Jerome. 'I'd know it anywhere. The ice cream van.'

The strange van was now turning on to a road that wound off the motorway and up into the mountains.

'What a piece of luck,' said Tabby-Jack. 'It's coming this way.'

They watched the van roll slowly uphill. It stopped for a moment, coughing and groaning, and then it moved off the road and parked on a piece of rough ground beside the woods.

'Come on, cats,' yelled Jerome. 'We'll reach it in no time.'

Tudor's heart began to thump. If Delilah were a prisoner in the ice cream van, how were they going to rescue her from the mad, white-haired creature? A woman strong enough to kill tigers.

# 8

# The Prisoner

Delilah has not been frightened since she was a kitten. Now she remembers the sensations of pain, confusion and loneliness.

She is in an awful place: dark and poisonous-smelling. She is trapped in a glass box with a tiny hole at the top for air. Sometimes the woman with white hair drops a dead mouse through the hole. Delilah refuses to eat them. She does not eat the kill of other creatures. Once the woman lifted the lid of Delilah's box to give her a saucer of water, but Delilah scratched her hand so badly that the woman dropped the saucer. It smashed on Delilah's glass floor, spilling the water, and now her tail is wet and cold and bits of broken china surround her like a minefield, so she cannot move.

Delilah can see no way of escape. She peers out at shelves of pickled things in bottles. They are a horrid dead colour and make

Delilah feel sick. At the end of this gloomy
room, candlelight flickers over a wall of
strange black and white photographs. The
largest of these is in a golden frame and it
shows a man with a gun, wearing an upside-
down pudding bowl on his head, and sitting
on an elephant. In front of the elephant lies a
dead tiger.

Delilah gives a growl of sympathy and then
she spies those silly little dogs that caused all
the trouble. They sounded frightening when
the dishwasher was turned on, but they are
hollow things with batteries inside; a clever
trick, not magic at all. Delilah spits in disgust.

An ugly face pushes itself up to her box and grins, showing huge dog-like teeth. 'Caught you, didn't I?' laughs Bianca Bono.

Delilah spits again.

This only makes Bianca howl with joy. 'What am I going to do with you? That's the question.'

Is she asking herself or Delilah? Delilah tries to turn her back on the woman but the broken china is too painful. Bianca moves round and makes Delilah look at her.

'You're a bit of a problem, you are,' Bianca tells her. 'I could get rid of you entirely, I want you to know that, but I'm squeamish and, anyway, I want to save you for my Grand Performance.'

Delilah huddles down and glares at Bianca, hoping to frighten her. But the woman seems only to find her funny.

'Ha! Ha!' Bianca gives a bitter laugh. 'I'm not scared of you, witch-cat! You can only make dogspells. But that's why I've got to keep you a prisoner, while my Ogre goes to work. My Ogre is a monster-dog. I've reared him on superfluous kittens, see, and he loves the taste. He'd die for a bowl of roast cat, and cats is what he's going to get.'

Delilah is so appalled her fur stiffens like the

spines of a hedgehog.

'Hundreds and hundreds of cats!' hoots Bianca. 'Thousands and millions of them.' Her dreadful features come so close that the glass is misted with her breath. 'Every cat in the whole wide world,' she whispers venomously, and behind the wall of yellow teeth Delilah watches a pale tongue move in the dark hollow of her mouth. Delilah closes her eyes against the dreadful sight.

Now Bianca changes her tune. She wanders away from Delilah's box and begins to sob. 'Bertram, my love, my heart is broken. Who will mend it?'

A fit of weeping follows this cry from the heart and Delilah thinks: so the woman has a weakness after all. A kitten could break into that wicked soul and change it. But will Tudor know what to do, even if he finds her?

Bianca dries her tears and swoops back to Delilah. 'I don't underestimate you, my girl. You really are a witch, aren't you? I've seen the results of your work. My friend, Olga, had a demon of a dog, but you shrunk him, didn't you, you fiend? Just for showing interest in a pretty Siamese. He wouldn't have hurt it. But you hurt him. Now he's the size of a mole and no use to anyone.'

Delilah opens one eye. She can't resist a purr of satisfaction.

This infuriates Bianca who screams, 'Well, you're not going to shrink my Ogre. I may not be a witch but I'm a clever conjuror. I'm going to put you in a hat and keep you there until every cat in the world has gone. And then I'll bring you out, with a wave of my wand and a flourish of ribbons and stars, and everyone will cry, 'Bravo, Bianca!' And my Bertram will be avenged because there'll be no more cats except for you, and you'll be mine; my special Grand Finale! Ha! Ha! Ha!'

Delilah's eyes widen with shock. Bianca is now holding a long black wand in one hand and a large shiny hat in the other. Delilah knows that something dreadful is going to happen.

And it does!

The lid of her glass box is blown away and she is sucked up into a terrible darkness.

# 9

# Following Tabby-Jack

'You look terrible,' Annie said when Edward walked into her kitchen next morning.

'I didn't sleep a wink,' Edward confessed.

They had spent the previous evening hunting for Delilah. They had visited all the neighbours, searched the woods, had wandered through the town, scanning the streets and peering down every alley; even Mr and Mrs Pugh had joined in because Edward was so upset.

But Annie had noticed that Edward's heart wasn't really in it. He didn't expect to find Delilah. He was convinced that she had been stolen by the creature with white hair.

'I can't find Tudor this morning, if that makes you feel any better,' Annie said.

'Of course it doesn't. Something odd is going on, Annie. Look how the cats behaved yesterday, and what about that awful delivery man. Normal people don't go round flinging fireworks at cats.'

'There's another thing,' Annie said, throwing herself into the mystery. 'Our dishwasher was really yours. Perhaps someone *meant* Delilah to get trapped in it. Perhaps there was a noise in it that frightened Tudor. A noise we couldn't hear.'

'So your stupid kitten comes and gets Delilah to investigate it for him.'

'Exactly. But please don't call him stupid. He's just young and timid.'

The doorbell rang before their conversation could turn into an argument. They heard Mrs Watkin talking to someone on the doorstep and then the kitchen door opened and a policeman wheeled in the dishwasher.

'Isn't it wonderful?' cried Mrs Watkin, hovering round the policeman. 'I've got my dishwasher back.'

'Where was it?' asked Annie, giving Edward a hopeful look.

'In the woods at the bottom of Madog's mountain,' said Mrs Watkin. 'And the white van was just a few feet away. It was stolen apparently.'

'Is the . . . was the dishwasher . . . empty?' asked Edward, approaching the machine with an air of fearful anticipation.

'Quite empty, lad,' replied the policeman. 'We'll continue to search for the thief, of course, Mrs Watkin, but seeing you've recovered your property and considering the "person" was disguised to the extent that we don't know if it was male or female . . . !'

'Yes,' said Mrs Watkin, unsure of what she was agreeing to. 'Thank you very much.'

The policeman nodded, said 'Ta-ra, then,' and retreated.

Annie and Edward stared hard at the dishwasher while Mrs Watkin manoeuvred it into place.

'See if you can open it, Mum,' Annie said.

Mrs Watkin pulled open the door. She closed it with a click, and opened it again. 'Perfect,' she declared. 'Nothing wrong with it at all. Peculiar, isn't it?'

Edward seemed to be in a trance. 'He was just trying it on,' he murmured. 'When the thief came to your door, Mrs Watkin, he said, "Having trouble with your dishwasher, dear?" He watched it being delivered, you see and knew it had come to the wrong house.'

'What makes you think the person was a he?' asked Annie.

'Ssssh!' Edward hissed. 'I can't keep calling it "it", can I? Where was I? Oh, yes. Well, he

76

probably knew that you'd want to try out your dishwasher pretty soon. So he waited and saw Delilah run in to your house and was quite sure she had gone to investigate the dishwasher.'

'Why?' Annie and her mother asked together.

'I don't know, do I?' Edward shouted.

'Edward, there's no need to be rude.' Mrs Watkin was losing patience. 'I know you're both upset about your cats but there's probably a very simple explanation.'

Edward ground his teeth, quietly. Pictures were forming in his mind; he described them to Annie. 'The thief took Delilah away locked in the dishwasher, then he abandoned the white van, dragged the dishwasher into the woods, pulled Delilah out and put her in a box. Then he got into another vehicle with Delilah which was standing nearby, and drove off. Thieves always change cars. She's special, my Delilah, and I mean really special. I think the thief wants to use her for some secret and diabolical purpose.'

Annie was about to suggest they search the town again when Tabby-Jack leapt through the cat-flap and stood miaowing loudly at them.

'Now what?' sighed Mrs Watkin. 'I wish I could get on.'

'It's Tabby-Jack,' Annie exclaimed. 'And he's trying to tell us something.'

Tabby-Jack leapt out through the cat-flap.

'He wants us to follow him,' Annie said.

'Yes! Yes! Yes!' cried Edward. 'Let's fetch our bikes.'

'No,' said Mrs Watkin. 'I don't mind you playing in the field at the back but . . .'

'We are not *playing*!' both children said vehemently.

'This is serious, Mum,' Annie went on. 'How would it be if Dilys Daybreak went with us? After all Tabby-Jack's her cat. And she's in the fourth year at High School.'

Mrs Watkin considered this. 'Yes,' she said, at last. 'But stay together, and leave your bikes behind. The roads are very dangerous.'

The children groaned and Mrs Watkin went to telephone Mrs Daybreak.

Ten minutes later Dilys Daybreak arrived with her boyfriend Walt. Walt had shaved his head rather unevenly and wore an earring but when he told Mrs Watkin that he wanted to be a bank manager she found it easier to believe that he was a responsible sort of boy. Dilys was tall, blonde and sensible. She was

kind to younger children and adored her cat. She would have walked miles to save Tabby-Jack and it didn't take long to convince her that the tabby cat wanted to show them something important.

'Edward's cat has been stolen and we think Tabby-Jack knows where she is,' Annie explained.

By now Tabby-Jack was showing signs of intense agitation: howling, trilling, leaping at their legs and then retreating with arched back and quivering tail.

'Let's go then,' said Walt.

The smart tabby set a brisk pace. Soon

Annie, Edward, Dilys and Walt were running. Whenever they had to stop for a rest, Tabby-Jack looked back anxiously, allowed them a few minutes' breather, and then leapt ahead with even greater speed.

They reached the road that led up Madog's mountain and Walt insisted on a five-minute break before the climb.

Tabby-Jack allowed them only two minutes.

'You'd think Walt would be fitter than us, wouldn't you?' Annie whispered to Edward.

'His boots are heavy.' Edward felt he had to defend a member of his own sex.

Tabby-Jack had now jumped through the bars of a farm gate. The others climbed it, Walt making heavy weather of the job. They followed the cat along a narrow sheep-track until they reached a road that led through an oak wood. Parked on the grass in front of the trees was a tall pink van. You could tell that it had once been an ice cream van, but now it was decorated with strange pictures. Inside a circle of stars were the words:

### BIANCA BONO
### FORTUNE-TELLER

As the children stood gazing at this

mysterious vehicle, three cats crept round the side: one ginger, one pure white and one jet black kitten.

'Tudor,' cried Annie, scooping up the kitten and smothering him with kisses. 'You brave kitten. Have you found Delilah?'

Before the kitten could even attempt to explain, a door in the side of the van opened and an old woman with a cloud of white hair peered out at them. She wore a long velvet cloak, black chiffon trousers and gold-coloured sandals.

'What d'you want?' snarled this horrible-looking crone, curling her top lip to reveal a row of huge yellow teeth.

Annie was standing right in front of the door, and because she couldn't think of anything else to say, she mumbled, 'I want my fortune told!'

# 10

# Annie and the Fortune-teller

'Five quid!' croaked Bianca Bono.

'You must be joking,' jeered Walt. 'This van is illegal. Your left rear light's been smashed.'

The woman growled; her narrow black eyes darted over the row of cats and children, and settled on Tabby-Jack.

'Recognise the sandals?' Edward whispered to Annie.

Annie did. The last time she had seen them, her mum's dishwasher was being wheeled away.

'Two quid then?' said the fortune-teller, still glaring at Tabby-Jack.

'Done!' said Walt. He laid two pounds in the woman's wrinkled palm and prodded Annie forward.

Annie looked beseechingly at Dilys, who said, 'Can I come in, too, Miss . . .'

'*Mrs* Bono,' snapped the woman, turning

her back.

'Ed and me'll stay out here,' said Walt, giving the girls a broad wink, 'and have a scout around,' he added in an undertone.

'No cats!' screeched Bianca Bono as Annie was about to climb on the van.

Annie handed Tudor to Edward. Dilys gave her hand an encouraging squeeze and they stepped up into the fortune-teller's strange parlour.

Black velvet curtains had been drawn across the windows and the only light came from a row of flickering candles on a shelf. Beneath the candles, another shelf held huge jars of wicked-looking liquids and horrid pale, floating things. Annie's stomach lurched. She looked for a place to sit down.

At the far end of the van there was a low couch covered with a Persian rug, and against the wall two chairs stood either side of a small table. One of the chairs was high-backed and comfortable, the other small and hard. Annie was told to sit on the small hard chair, Dilys on the couch.

When Annie sat down she found herself facing the wall above Dilys. It was covered in photographs, mostly of a tall white-haired man with a wand. In some of the pictures he

was holding a top hat and a white rabbit, in others he was making flowers, birds, handkerchiefs, ribbons and stars erupt from boxes.

'My father was the world's greatest conjuror,' explained Bianca, following Annie's gaze. 'His name was the Great Nimblini.'

'How amazing,' said Annie, 'and can you do . . . ?'

'Of course,' said the fortune-teller. 'But he was a master. I merely . . . follow.' Dead-white bony fingers fluttered over the table and Annie caught the glitter of gold on nails that resembled long claws. Then she noticed a photograph of a man with black hair and a gun, sitting in a box on top of an elephant.

'And was he a conjuror too?' Annie asked.

'That is my husband, Mr Bono,' said Bianca solemnly. 'Bertram Bono on his Nepalese elephant.' She took a pack of cards from a wooden box on the table and sat in the high-backed chair opposite Annie. 'He was a great hunter and I loved him more than life itself.'

A grave silence followed this pronouncement. Annie looked helplessly at Dilys, who asked, 'Then is Mr Bono . . . ?'

'He was eaten!' Bianca savagely declared. 'By a tiger. Every scrap gone! Dragged off! Mauled! Evil, diabolic fiends.' She leaned across the table and with a waft of foul-smelling breath, confided, 'That's why I can't abide cats. I'd kill 'em every one, if I had my way.'

Annie wanted to say that this was hardly fair and that she expected Mr Bono deserved his awful fate as tigers were an endangered species, but she could only bring herself to mutter, 'Oh, dear!'

Dilys followed this with, 'What a shame,'

which seemed hardly adequate, seeing she was a member of WWF, but was all she could manage.

'Once I thought I'd die without my Bertram,' Bianca sighed, oh so sadly, 'but then I thought, no, I shall dedicate my life to avenging him.' She cleared her throat, ordered, 'Let's get on!', and began to shuffle her cards.

Annie sat very still, mesmerised by the long fingers and the silky clicking of the cards. And she began to wonder why she was here at all, in this dark, scary place that smelled of mildew and very old scent. And where was Delilah, anyway? Was the fortune-teller keeping her a prisoner in one of the mysterious trunks piled in a corner? Or was she already . . . ? Annie glanced at the jars of pickled limbs and swallowed hard. On top of the trunks there was a square glass-sided box, empty except for a few dead mice and some broken china. There was something familiar and sad about the glass box, it seemed like a sort of clue. Annie was trying to work it out when she saw two tiny bronze-coloured dogs. They were hanging from a nail by a thin gold chain.

'They're my little dishwasher dogs,' Bianca

said proudly. 'They're only small but they've got batteries inside them and they have horrible growls when I put them in a dishwasher. My own invention. Aren't I clever? Ha! Ha! Ha!'

Annie could see it all now. Tudor must have heard those tiny dogs growling in the depths of the dishwasher. He'd run to fetch Delilah and she had bravely entered the machine to deal with them. But somehow this horrible old woman had fixed the dishwasher so that it had become a trap. Delilah had been caught and stolen away. But why had Bianca chosen Delilah? Perhaps the wise and famous cat was a threat to some secret plan? Annie wondered if Bianca could do things to people too. She looked at Dilys to make sure she hadn't vanished into the gloom at the end of the van.

'Here, stop dreaming and take one!' Bianca held out a fan of cards, face down.

Annie took a card. It was the Queen of Hearts. 'Is that good?' she asked.

'Depends, doesn't it,' replied the fortune-teller, showing her frightening teeth again.

Outside the pink van, Walt tapped the bonnet and listened. Edward crawled beneath the van, and scanned the underside for a box or a wire crate that might be attached to the chassis. Walt climbed on the bonnet and knocked on the roof, while Edward gave his special Delilah call, as quietly as he could. But if Delilah was a prisoner she either could not or would not reply.

'Come and have a look at this, Ed!' Walt had walked round the back of the van.

Edward scrambled out and saw the tiger's skin. 'That's disgusting,' he said. 'It's bad enough to kill a tiger, but to hang its skin up like that . . .'

Inside the van Annie and Dilys looked at each other. They knew what all the ghostly tappings and bangings were, of course. Bianca Bono, without taking her eyes from the cards, said, 'They won't find it.'

'Find what?' Annie ventured in a small voice.

'IT!' The fortune-teller's small black eyes focused hard on Annie and she repeated, 'IT! You know what I mean. They won't find anything.' And she gave a horrible witchy sort of cough that made Annie's scalp tingle.

'Delilah always answers,' Edward said miserably as he tried to wipe mud and black grease off his jeans. 'Perhaps she's been . . .'

'Don't even think of it, boy! C'mon, we'll have a look in the wood.' Walt waded into the mass of undergrowth beneath the trees. Edward followed hopefully. After a few moments they found themselves looking at a small wired enclosure. On the other side of the wire sat the most enormous dog they had ever seen.

'What the . . .' said Walt.

'It's a monster,' whispered Edward.

Although the dog was huge and very ugly it came towards them wagging its tail and panting as though it had just been exercising vigorously. Then it gave a pathetic yelp and stood on its hind legs, resting its front paws on the wire.

The two boys backed away and Edward said, 'I think it's hungry.'

'Too right it's hungry,' Walt agreed.

At that moment the four cats crept out from the trees behind Walt and Edward. The dog gave a deep, hollow bark and roared round its enclosure, growling and snarling. At length it flung itself at the wire, right in front of the cats, who shot off in all directions.

'Get down, you brute.' Walt stood his ground.

The monster dog gnashed its teeth, bits of foam flew out of its great mouth and dribbled down its dappled jaws.

All at once something unspeakable, unbearable and almost unthinkable crossed Edward's mind.

'You don't think it's eaten Delilah, do you?' he whispered.

'Looks as if it could,' Walt admitted tactlessly. 'Looks illegal too. I bet it hasn't got a licence. C'mon.' He marched back to the pink van and rapped on the door.

'D'you think you should?' said Edward. 'I mean Bianca Bono might be in a trance or something.'

'Trance? She's a fortune-teller, not a medium,' said Walt. 'It's time those girls were out of there. I don't like the set–up.' He rapped on the side of the van and shouted, 'Time's up.'

The door flew open and Bianca Bono glared down at him. 'I haven't finished,' she snarled.

'Well, I'm sure the girls have had enough, thank you very much,' said Walt.

Annie and Dilys sidled past the fortune-teller. 'Thanks very much,' they said, leaping happily into the fresh air.

91

'We found a dog in there.' Walt waved a thumb in the direction of the wood. 'Is it yours?'

'Mind your own business,' grunted Bianca.

'I hope you've got a licence for it,' Walt went on. 'They're illegal, dogs like that, you know. Fighting dogs. Dangerous, they are!'

'That's not a fighting dog,' Bianca told him with a sneer. 'He's my Ogre, he doesn't hurt people – unless I tell him to. He's got a very special job to do and by the time he's finished the world will never be the same again. And yes, I have got a licence. So there!' She stuck out a warty looking tongue.

Edward was a determined boy however. 'Have you stolen my cat, Delilah?' he asked.

'What?' screeched the crone.

'I think you have,' Edward said, gaining courage. 'In fact I *know* you have. I just know it. You stole Mrs Watkin's dishwasher and you knew Delilah was inside it.'

The fortune-teller's face had turned bright purple. 'Get away,' she cried, flinging her arms out at them. 'Go on, before I turn you into handkerchiefs.'

But Edward was in full steam now. 'I recognise your sandals. Annie does too.' Annie nodded. 'And even if you did give back the van and the dishwasher, you can still be arrested for stealing a valuable cat.'

Bianca Bono emitted a scream like a siren. 'No, I can't,' she shrieked. 'You'll never find that horrible witchy cat. I've heard about your Delilah shrinking dogs. Well, she's not going to shrink my Ogre. I've reared him to eat cats, and that's not against the law. One of these days he's going to eat every stinking cat in the whole wide world. And my darling Bertram will be AVENGED!' She gave such a high-pitched cackle the girls had to cover their ears, and even Walt and Edward retreated.

'So you'd better get away from here,' the fortune-teller lowered her voice to a venomous mutter, 'or I'll let my Ogre gobble up those rotten little beasts right now.' She pointed a finger, quivering with hatred, at the four cats who were peeping fearfully from behind the children.

The children each gathered up a cat and ran; or rather Annie, Edward and Dilys ran. Walt just walked rapidly. Jerome was clinging to his neck, his heart thumping against Walt's heart.

## 11

# Defeated!

'Poor old boy,' Walt comforted the big tom. 'I won't let her get you.'

Bianca's Ogre had given Jerome the fright of his life. He knew that he, of all cats, should not have lost his nerve so easily. He would lose his reputation for courage in the face of the enemy. But it was so unusual and so pleasant to be carried. He could not bring himself to break away from Walt.

Dilys, carrying Tabby-Jack, slowed down to keep Walt company. 'Walt, you were brave,' she said.

Walt's heart swelled. 'Edward played his part,' he admitted.

'It's his cat we're looking for.'

'Doubt if we'll find it now,' said Walt. 'D'you think this cat would stay with me? It's a nice old thing.'

'I'm sure it would,' Dilys told him. 'Uncle Harold can't wait to get rid of it.'

Edward had heard the conversation behind him. He felt close to despair. He tried to pretend that Rose was Delilah and buried his face in the soft fur between her ears.

'Bianca Bono is quite mad,' Annie said. 'She's trying to kill cats just because her silly old husband got eaten by a tiger. She's too much of a coward to get back at the really big cats, the tigers and leopards and things. So she's taking it out on the little ones.' She realised this was not helping Edward. 'I'm so sorry, Edward,' she said. 'But we *will* find Delilah. A cat like her doesn't disappear for ever. She's too marvellous. I mean she's a witch, isn't she? If she's Bianca's prisoner, she'll escape somehow.'

'I don't know,' Edward moaned. 'Don't forget, Delilah can only work on dogs. She has no power at all over humans. Oh, Annie, I feel so – so defeated!'

'You mustn't give up hope,' insisted Annie. 'Bianca's just a common fortune-teller, a conjuror. She's not an enchantress. And Delilah's very, very clever.'

'Yes.' Edward managed a smile, but he didn't say another word until they reached Annie's house.

A magnificent lunch had been spread on the

Watkins' kitchen table. Annie's mother could always be relied upon in times of crisis. As soon as she saw the children coming up the front path without Delilah she had run to the freezer to get Edward's favourite dessert: choc-chip ice cream with bananas.

'Wow!' Edward exclaimed, somewhat comforted for a moment.

Mrs Watkin provided four saucers of milk for the cats while the children waded into beefburgers, cold ham, beans, salad, pizza and chips. Mr Watkin played his latest composition on a tape recorder to entertain everyone during the meal, but in spite of all this Annie noticed that Edward wasn't eating.

'Is it the music, or . . . ?' she asked him.

'No, it isn't the music,' said Edward. 'Excuse me.' And he ran out of the house.

'He's taking it very hard,' Walt remarked.

'I don't think he'll be able to eat anything

ever again,' said Annie, 'if he doesn't get Delilah back.'

'A moggy is a moggy,' Walt said. 'We'll get him another one and he'll forget all about old Delilah.'

Annie was almost stung into making a rude reply but she knew that when Walt had a cat of his own he would understand.

After the meal Dilys and Walt thanked the Watkins heartily and took Tabby-Jack, Jerome and Rose home. Perhaps it would be more truthful to say the cats appeared to be accompanying the teenagers, for they were frequently diverted by bits of paper, leaves, crisp packets and all manner of wind-blown things. Unknown to Walt and Dilys, the cats were passing messages.

Alone with Tudor, Annie looked into the kitten's mossy eyes and asked, 'I suppose you cats couldn't rescue Delilah, could you?'

The kitten blinked. He couldn't, of course, tell Annie what the other cats had planned before they left. Annie was looking very hard at him. Did she guess?

'No,' said Annie. 'I'm being silly. You're too small and too nervous for such a dangerous mission.'

But Annie was wrong.

# 12

# A Thousand Cats

Three cats had not been idle. A message had been passed through hedges, through cat-flaps, gates and windows. It had been sung over fields and gardens, roofs and trees. The word was out:

DELILAH, A PRISONER.
RESCUE TONIGHT.

Devoted cat owners began to notice that their pets were behaving strangely; they were edgy, tense, alert to the smallest sound. They ate voraciously, as if preparing for some long and arduous adventure. They sharpened their claws, avoided human contact and anxiously watched the sky.

When the moon had reached its zenith three cats and a kitten met in the Pughs' orchard. Tudor was almost faint with apprehension. All day nightmares had chased through his mind. He hadn't slept a wink.

'I'm so tired,' he mewed. 'I don't think I can walk all that way again.'

'You'll have to,' Jerome said sternly. 'Every cat is needed. Every one, especially you!'

Tudor felt the big tom's disapproval like a weight on his shoulders.

'Bear up, Tudor,' said Tabby-Jack. 'Can you imagine life without Delilah?'

'No,' Tudor confessed in a whisper.

'He's a brave kitten.' Rose's soft green eyes were full of encouragement. 'And he's going to do just fine.'

They stepped out on to the pavement in single file. Jerome in the lead, Tabby-Jack following close behind and then Tudor. Rose came last, to keep an eye on the kitten. The little troupe walked swiftly beside the road and, as they travelled, Tudor became aware of hushed movements all around him, as though whispers were pouring through gates and hedges, round corners and out of windows, slipping over walls, down drainpipes and trees. The whispers were cats; cats of every description moving like a silky stream that grew and grew into a great river of shining, flowing, silent bodies. And the black kitten was filled with wonder and then with pride to

think that Delilah, his Delilah, had caused this torrent of loyalty and devotion, this great throng of worshipping cats.

As they crept up the mountain road, Tudor looked back at the gleaming ribbon of cats behind him and thought it far more wonderful and certainly more beautiful than Motorway. How many creatures had Delilah helped? he wondered. How many had she saved? And how had she found the time? He had thought himself to be the only kitten in her life, yet there had been hundreds, thousands more, for they were coming from miles away. He could see them swarming over the fields and surging up Madog's mountain like a great wind. He forgot his exhaustion and his fear and allowed himself to be carried along by the heavy tide of cats.

Still in the lead, Jerome left the road, jumped through a five-barred gate and began to run along the mountain track. The others followed. Excitement rippled along their ranks. They were getting closer to Delilah. Every cat was running now, some even leaping in anticipation. Tudor lost sight of Jerome and Tabby-Jack; he felt that at any moment he would be trampled by the great rush of cats. But, whenever he stopped in panic, to stare at the bobbing, racing, slinking army, the white cat would be at his side to give him a lick or a purr of reassurance.

On the last of these occasions Rose said, 'We're there, Tudor. You've done well.' And Tudor noticed that the army had slowed down. He tried to look over their heads but was so much smaller than any of the cats close to him he could only see the moon perched upon a lacework of tall trees. Rose nudged him. 'You're wanted at the front,' she said. 'Come on!' Gently she butted a fat tortoiseshell standing in his way. The big cat stepped back and Rose repeated the procedure with the next cat. 'Make way, please,' her clear musical voice rang softly through the night. 'Delilah's foster son is here.' And Tudor found himself pacing down an avenue of tall creatures, while eyes that gleamed in every shade between silver, gold, green and blue silently followed him. By the time he reached Tabby-Jack he felt dizzy from the glare.

He found himself looking at the mysterious ice cream van. Moonlight gave the golden figures on its side a dull glitter, and Tudor felt terribly afraid for Delilah. He knew without a doubt that she was inside the van. The sense and smell of her was even stronger now. Was it possible? Could he hear her, very, very faintly?

'What do we do now?' he asked Tabby-Jack.

There was no time for his friend to reply. A terrible sound echoed over their heads and a roaring, howling monster bounded in front of the van. Its huge teeth were bared in a ghastly grin, its mean bloodshot eyes glared hungrily along the ranks of cats and a growl rattled in its throat as deep and dark as doom. This was a creature that roamed through every cat's nightmare.

A profound stillness descended on the cats and beneath the monster's voice, Tudor could hear the drumming of a thousand terrified hearts.

# 13

## Tudor's Finest Hour

'I'm to blame,' Jerome muttered miserably. 'I should have guessed that the woman would set her monster loose at night.'

'But there are many of us,' said Tabby-Jack. 'Perhaps if just a few diverted the dog . . .'

'Sacrificed themselves, you mean?' Jerome looked interested, but Rose gasped, 'Oh, no. How would we chose?'

'Volunteers,' Jerome told her.

'It's too much to ask,' she said gravely.

They gazed helplessly at the great dog whose growls were, if anything, becoming deeper and more menacing. It lowered its great head and began to approach them.

A petrified hiss resounded through the sea of cats and a thousand backs arched in horror.

It was then that the two brothers noticed the chain clipped to the dog's collar. They could see the end of the chain looped round a post a few feet away from the van. Beside the post the chain lay coiled into a dark mound. It could have been a mile long. How many lives would be lost before the dog had run that distance and was finally drawn back?

'A dog that size has used most of its energy to grow,' Tabby-Jack remarked thoughtfully.

'How does that help?' asked Jerome.

'There probably wasn't much left for developing its brain,' Tabby-Jack told him. 'In other words it's quite possibly very stupid.'

'But hungry,' Rose observed.

'And strong,' Tudor added, 'and coming closer.'

'So,' yowled Tabby-Jack, throwing caution to the wind, 'we must act fast and I mean now. I know you're bigger and braver, Jerome. But leave this to me. I'm the fastest cat I know.'

'And maybe the cleverest,' Tudor murmured as Tabby-Jack sprang towards the van, right under the nose of the astonished monster. In a split second it had recovered, however, and leapt after the tabby cat with a yelp of fury.

There followed such a terrifying chase, such a claw-biting, chilling game that it would live in Tudor's memory for ever. A monument to cats' bravery and intelligence.

Tabby-Jack anticipated the monster's every move. When the dog was speeding round the back of the van, Tabby-Jack would nip round a corner and hide behind a wheel, and out he would spring when the dog had passed. If the monster got too close, he would leap under the van, staying only long enough to confuse the beast. He knew he must keep going in one direction so that the chain would wind round and round the van without the dog realising what was happening.

'Oh, my,' breathed Rose. 'What courage!'

But the fortune-teller's dog had worked out that there might be just enough space beneath the van for him, too, and the next time Tabby-Jack went under, so did he.

There was a sudden squeal of pain. The audience held its breath and watched the shadows beneath the pink van. They heard a low crunching. Tudor began to close his eyes, but Rose whispered, 'Look!' as the tabby crawled out into the moonlight. For a moment his eyes gleamed out at them and then he vanished round a corner as the monster dragged himself from under the van. But as cat and dog circled once again Tudor noticed that Tabby-Jack was limping. It was obvious that he could hardly bear to put one back foot on the ground. Wounded and in pain, he was at a terrible disadvantage. Now the monster's jaws were only inches from the cat and, with every bound, the gap between them became smaller and smaller.

He can't go on, thought Tudor, turning his head into Rose's soft fur. He's too tired, too hurt. What can we do? He peeped back just in time to see Tabby-Jack stumble and fall on his side, all the breath knocked out of him. The brave tabby looked fearlessly at his executioner's ugly muzzle and waited.

The monster gave a howl of triumph and reared over his helpless victim. The silent spectators froze with horror. You could have heard a whisker drop. Savouring the moment, the dog waited a second before lunging forward for his meal. Instead there was a snap and roar of stunned fury as the chain went taut.

The nearest thing to a cheer resounded over the mountain fields as Tabby-Jack rolled clear of the dog's paws and slowly got to his feet.

Beside him the van door opened and a hooded figure stood on the threshold. Behind her, candlelight shivered in the sudden gust of air. Bianca Bono surveyed the sea of cats with a look of horror and disbelief.

When they saw that the dog was now helpless some of the cats pressed forward; they jumped on the bonnet of the van, a few even climbed on to the roof. An eerie wailing broke out and then, with one voice, they all cried, 'DEEE-LI-LAAAH!'

Bianca stared about her like someone who could not wake from a nightmare. She opened her mouth and screamed, but nothing could be heard above the howling of a thousand cats.

The fortune-teller covered her ears and sank on to her step, shaking her head from side to side so that her hood fell back, revealing the cloud of white hair.

'Shall we rush her?' asked an elegant Siamese.

'No,' said Jerome. 'It's a delicate situation. Negotiation is the only way now. Otherwise we might never see Delilah again. Tudor, the time has come for you to play your part.'

'My part?' mewed Tudor.

'Delilah is your foster mother,' Tabby-Jack reminded him.

'Yes,' Tudor agreed in a frightened whisper. He could feel the glowing eyes of his three friends, and behind them all the other eyes, turned in his direction. Waiting for him to act.

'But . . .' he swallowed. 'I don't know what to do.'

'You will,' said Rose kindly. Even she, it seemed, could not excuse him from the awful thing that he must do. But what could it be?

'Move closer to the woman,' Tabby-Jack advised, 'and perhaps you'll learn what to do.'

How could Tudor refuse a cat who had already risked his life. He inched forward. 'Closer,' said Jerome. Tudor gave a little run, then stopped. The white-haired woman was looking straight at him. Her face was grim enough to shrivel his bones. Behind him the cats called, 'Go on. Good lad! Don't give up, now. Remember, Delilah!' And thinking only of her, he walked forward, slowly but steadily until he reached the hem of the woman's cloak. Her shadowy face was high, high above him and yet he learned from the twisted mouth and the glitter in her black eyes, that she was not angry. She was AFRAID! Bianca Bono was the most frightened human that he had ever seen. This multitude of cats had terrified her, just as the dark spaces of the night terrified him. And Tudor found that he was sorry for the poor shuddering creature, so sorry that he forgot his own terror and knew what he had to do.

Dangerous it may be, he thought. Even foolhardy. Perhaps he would not live through it. But it couldn't be helped. Tudor flexed his tail, tensed his muscles and leapt into Bianca Bono's dark lap.

There was an expectant hush.

Tudor felt the old woman stiffen. He found a tiny purr and used it to reassure her. A bony hand appeared and touched his head; it moved between his ears and down his back, and

Tudor's purr crescendoed into a rhythmic hum of pleasure.

A thousand cats gasped in disbelief.

'Are my eyes deceiving me?' murmured Tabby-Jack.

'He's never purring,' said Jerome, 'not in a situation like that.'

'The power of a kitten,' mused Rose. 'I've always known.'

'Don't speak too soon,' warned Jerome.

The fortune-teller held Tudor for a moment in both hands. Was she going to strangle him? No. She set him on the ground and went inside the van. No one could tell what would happen next.

Have I failed? Tudor wondered. Have a thousand cats followed us for nothing?

But Bianca's door did not close. In a moment she reappeared with a small table; she set this on the ground and flung a crimson cloth over it, then she stepped quickly inside the van and brought out a tall black hat, a velvet box and a wand.

The cats watched: some moved restlessly; others voiced their disappointment in loud catcalls. Where was Delilah?

Bianca Bono waved her wand and a dove swooped up into the moonlight. She opened the box and a cloud of stars flew out and settled on her wand. She shook the wand and the stars turned into a rainbow of coloured ribbons that coiled themselves into a pattern of flowers, then turned into handkerchiefs.

If Bianca Bono's audience had been human it would have applauded such clever conjuring. But the spectators were cats impatient to see their queen. If some of their number were impressed by the show of stars, handkerchiefs and ribbons, they were not going to admit it. They miaowed restlessly, argued and waved their tails. Small scuffles broke out and the leaders began to fear that the night would end in disaster.

Bianca had a routine, however. She could not reach the climax of her entertainment without first performing all the tricks that led up to it.

Only Tudor, too young to disguise his admiration, sat enthralled as the dove fluttered over him and a coloured star settled on his ear.

'How impressionable he is,' said Rose fondly.

'This is getting us nowhere,' grumbled Jerome.

'Wait,' said Tabby Jack. 'The top hat! I have a feeling about it.'

Mrs Bono had reached the crowning moment of her career. Even her father had not thought of the trick that she was about to perform. The stars, birds, ribbons and handkerchiefs had vanished and she stood motionless, her cloak wrapped round her like a statue, her head bent in concentration.

Tudor held his breath. He, too, had a feeling about the tall black hat; his fur prickled at the back of his neck, and his whiskers tingled.

The conjuror's daughter took up her wand in two pale hands. She held it very still a few inches above the hat. She shouted strange

114

words into the air, her big teeth gleaming, then, with one hand, she waved the stick across the upturned hat. A faint sound echoed inside it and it began to shake, to spin so fast that nothing could be seen of it, but a whirling spiral of dust. And then out of the spinning dust something soared into the air; something that fizzed and bristled with wild smoky fur, something with eyes like burning gold.

This whirling, screaming mass of fur landed with a thump, its four legs planted squarely upon the conjuror's table.

It was Delilah, and she was FURIOUS!

# 14

## Delilah and the Ogre

Bianca Bono would never know that, at that moment, her life hung by a thread; that if the tiny kitten at her feet had not spoken, her career as conjuror and fortune-teller might have ended.

For as the enraged and vengeful Delilah turned on her kidnapper, Tudor cried, 'No, Mama!'

Delilah hesitated. She peered down into the shadows and found her foster son. 'Tudor?' she called.

'It's me, Mama,' said Tudor. 'Don't hurt the human. She brought you back for me.'

'Tudor,' Delilah said softly. 'You brave, wonderful kitten.'

Her words changed his life. He did not know why he made his next request. He had no knowledge of Bianca's past. 'Tell her we're not tigers, Mama,' he said.

Delilah regarded her foster kitten

thoughtfully. 'We are certainly not tigers,' she said, and turning to Bianca Bono, she repeated very forcibly, '*We are not tigers.*'

Perhaps Bianca Bono understood, for she inclined her head a little towards the amazing yellow-eyed creature, and then she murmured, 'Not tigers,' and sat back on her step, in a kind of trance.

Delilah leapt from the table to delirious cries of 'Dee-li-laah! Deee-li-laaah!' And Tudor found himself thumped and jostled by an army of triumphant cats, who leapt to welcome Delilah and pay her their respects. He managed to keep close to his foster mother by hiding in her thick, delicious-smelling fur. How safe he felt, how warm and happy. Peeping out, he saw Jerome and Tabby-Jack trying to make their way through the tumult of cats. Tudor could not understand their expressions. They should have been happy but they looked anxious and afraid. And then he saw what troubled them.

Throughout the fuss and fun the monster dog had been chewing through his chain. His huge teeth clamped themselves on the weak link once more, and the chain fell to the ground.

'Look out!' yelled Jerome as the deepest and

most fearful sound crescendoed from the monster's throat, and lowering his head like a great bull he charged straight at Delilah.

Tudor squealed and huddled deeper into Delilah's smoky fur, ready to die with her. But something was happening to the great cat. Her fur was alive with hot sounds, a sizzle that glowed and sent sparks into the night; they lit the monster's wicked muzzle and began to change it.

So this is it: thought Tudor. A dogspell!

And so it was.

Delilah's talents as a witch were legendary, but hundreds of the assembled cats had never actually seen a dogspell. It was something they would always remember. To watch a huge and fearsome enemy shrivel and shrink to the size of a squirrel was a delightful experience. The sight of a cat-crunching, kitten-munching Ogre being showered with burning stars that reduced him to a whimpering midget would give even the most timid cat a glow of confidence that would last a lifetime.

But as the dog (if you can call it that) ran whimpering to its mistress, Tudor dared to ask, 'What if she conjures it back into a monster, Mama?'

118

'Not a chance,' Delilah told him loftily. 'Conjuring is not magic. Conjuring is tricks. Magic is magic!'

And so it is, of course.

They left the fortune-teller still sitting on her step, still in a trance, patting her tiny dog and murmuring, 'Cats are not tigers, dear! They don't eat people!'

Which didn't reassure the wizened Ogre one little bit.

Well before dawn a milkman thought he saw the shadow of a cloud roll off Madog's mountain. He looked at the waning moon and wondered where the cloud had flown to. And when, towards the end of his round, he heard a swishing, whispering, rustling, a slithering through hedges, gates and fences, and a tapping, rapping, clattering and pattering of doors, bins and cat-flaps, he wondered where the wind was coming from; never guessing that a thousand cats were returning from a night on Madog's mountain; a night they would never forget.

## 15

# Jerome Finds a Home

Five cats did not go straight home after their adventure.

Delilah's imprisonment in a dishwasher and a top hat had made a mess of her fine fur, her tail was matted and her whiskers were a little limp. She really didn't want to greet Edward looking this way, so Rose, who had spent many informative hours in a beauty parlour, offered to give Delilah what she called 'a treatment'.

Jerome, Tabby-Jack and Tudor followed them into the orchard to watch this mysterious operation, and to make sure that Delilah looked her best when she got home.

So when Edward woke up and remembered his cat was still lost, Delilah was not at his door to cheer him up. He wandered across to Annie's house and found Dilys and Walt in the kitchen. Everyone was looking gloomy.

'It's the cats,' Annie told him. 'They've all disappeared again.'

'Catnapped by that horrible old fortune-teller, I bet,' said Dilys.

'Why would she do that?' asked Edward, who found it hard to believe that anyone would bother to steal such unremarkable cats. Delilah was, after all, special. He felt so miserable he almost said, there are plenty more in the pet shop, but he thought better of it.

'I can't stand it.' Walt banged his fist on the table. 'I love that ginger tom. I really love it!'

Edward was amazed.

Dilys said, 'Walt went to see Uncle Harold last night, didn't you, Walt? Gave him five pounds for Jerome, and Uncle Harold said the cat was Walt's now, for ever. Glad to get rid of it,' he said.

'I'd even thought of a new name,' said the distraught Walt. 'The Orange Dazzler. How about that?'

No one could think what to say. What was there to say? There was no Orange Dazzler Soon, Edward thought miserably, they would all be thinking up new names for new cats.

'I don't want to buy another cat,' he said

aloud, and his voice had a choky sound.

'You won't have to,' Annie told him. She seemed surprisingly happy.

'Yes, I will,' Edward argued without looking at her.

'No, you won't,' said Walt and Dilys.

Edward looked up and saw that they were all gazing into the garden. He flew to the window and looked over their shoulders.

Sitting in a row on Annie's lawn were five cats: one ginger, one tabby, one huge and grey, one white, and one very small black kitten.

'Tudor looks different,' Annie said. 'Sort of confident and proud. Something's happened to him.'

'I agree,' said Dilys.

But Edward had eyes for only one cat. 'Delilah!' he yelled, racing for the door, and the others followed very close behind him.

Mrs Pugh, dusting her bedroom furniture, looked out and saw an extraordinary muddle of cats and children, laughing, kissing, bouncing and hugging on the Watkins' lawn. Delilah and Tudor were back. There were some cats that you just couldn't lose, it seemed. She was pleased for Annie and Edward, of course, they could not help their wild behaviour, but those two teenagers were rather old to be romping about in such a silly way. 'It wasn't like that in my day,' Mrs Pugh said to herself.

Afterwards, Walt carried off his new cat like a prize, and the Orange Dazzler was so happy he did not even notice that Rose and Tabby-Jack had walked home together.

# 16

## Birds, Ribbons and Flowers

It is after midnight on a moonlit Friday.

Delilah is sitting on a pillar at the end of the Watkins' wall. Tudor has managed to squeeze in beside her.

'Mama,' says Tudor. 'What will become of the creature with white hair?'

'We'll see,' says Delilah. 'And don't call me Mama. You're nearly a tom. You may call me Delilah.'

'Thank you!' says Tudor.

A distant sound alerts them and a pink van comes rolling down the street. It stops in front of the cats and they see that birds, ribbons and flowers have been painted on the side. It looks very pretty. There are no men with guns, or teeth in the grass, and a top hat covers the broken heart.

Bianca gazes from the window of the driving-seat. She wears a funny lopsided smile and perched on her shoulder is a tiny dog.

'Good evening,' mews Tudor, but Delilah maintains a stony silence.

'Goodbye, dears!' Bianca Bono gives a little wave. 'Wish me luck!' And she drives away with a wistful smile, still covering those big, best-forgotten teeth.

The cats stare after the van and notice something. The tiger's skin has gone.

'What does it mean, Delilah?' asks Tudor.

'It means,' she tells him, 'that someone has given up trying to kill cats and is going to concentrate on conjuring. It also means that she will be much happier doing what she knows best. Now fetch me a rat.'

Without a moment's hesitation Tudor plunges joyfully into the dark spaces of the night.